HANSEL
AND
GRETEL

Retold by Ruth Belov Gross

Illustrated by Winslow Pinney Pels

SCHOLASTIC INC.

New York Toronto London Auckland Sydney

Once there was a little boy
and a little girl.
The boy's name was Hansel
and the girl's name was Gretel.
They lived with their father
and their stepmother
near a big forest.

Hansel and Gretel's father was a woodcutter.
He went into the forest every day
and chopped down trees.
Then he tried to sell the wood.

But times were bad.
People did not have enough money
to buy wood.
So very often the woodcutter and his family
did not have enough to eat.

One night the woodcutter could not sleep.
"Wife," he said, "things are very bad.
We have no food for ourselves
and hardly any food for our children.
I do not know what to do."

"I know what to do," his wife said.
"Early tomorrow morning
we will take the children deep into the forest
and leave them there.
They will never find their way home again."

"No, no!" said the woodcutter.
"I cannot leave my children in the forest."

"You must do it," his wife said.
"You must!
If you don't, we will all die of hunger."

Hansel and Gretel heard everything
their father and stepmother said.
Gretel began to cry.

"Don't cry, little sister," Hansel said.
"I will think of something."

Hansel waited until everyone was asleep.
Then he got out of bed.
He put on his coat and went outside.

There were hundreds of little pebbles
on the ground.
They looked very white and shiny
in the moonlight.
Hansel picked up as many pebbles
as he could. He put them in the pocket
of his coat and went back to bed.

Early the next morning, the stepmother
came to wake up Hansel and Gretel.
"Get up, lazybones," she said.
"We are going into the forest
to cut some wood."

She gave them each a little piece of bread.
"Here is your lunch," she said. "Don't lose it.
It is all you will get."

Hansel's pocket was full of pebbles.
So Gretel put her piece of bread
and Hansel's piece of bread
in her apron pocket.

Then they all set out for the forest.

When they had gone a little way,
Hansel stopped.
He turned around,
took a pebble out of his pocket,
and dropped it on the ground.

He stopped again and again.

"Why are you stopping and looking
around?" his father said.

"I am looking at my little white cat,
Father," Hansel said. "She is sitting on our
roof and wants to say good-bye to me."

"Fool!" the stepmother said.
"That is not your little white cat.
That is the sun shining on the chimney."

But Hansel was not really looking back
at his little white cat. He was really
dropping pebbles on the ground.
Every time he stopped,
he dropped another pebble.

At last Hansel and Gretel
and their father and stepmother
were deep in the forest.

The children helped to make a fire.
"The fire will keep you warm, my children,"
the woodcutter said.

"Sit down and rest by the fire,"
the stepmother said. "Your father and I
must go deeper into the forest
to chop some wood.
When our work is done, we will come back
and take you home."

Hansel and Gretel sat by the fire
as they were told.
When it was time for lunch,
they ate their little pieces of bread.

They waited and waited for their parents
to come back.
They grew so tired of waiting
that they fell asleep.

When the children woke up, it was dark.
"Now we will never find our way home,"
Gretel said.

"Don't cry, little sister," Hansel said.
"We will find our way home
as soon as the moon comes up."

Soon the moon was shining brightly.
It shone on the little white pebbles
that Hansel had dropped on the ground.
Now there was a path of white pebbles
for Hansel and Gretel to follow.
And now the children could
find their way home!

At last they were home.
The stepmother opened the door.
"You naughty children!" she said.
"Where have you been?
We thought you were never coming home."

A week or two later,
things were very bad again.
Again the woodcutter could not sleep.
"I do not know what to do,"
he said to his wife.

"I know what to do," his wife said.
"Tomorrow morning
we will take the children into the forest
and leave them there.
This time they will not find their way home.
I will see to that."

"No, no!" said the woodcutter.
"I cannot leave my children in the forest."

"You did it once," his wife said.
"Now you must do it again.
You must!
If you don't, we will all die of hunger."

Hansel and Gretel heard everything
their father and stepmother said.
Gretel began to cry.

"Don't cry, little sister," Hansel said.
"I will think of something."

Hansel waited until everyone was asleep.
He got out of bed, put on his coat,
and went to the door.
But he could not get outside.
The door was locked!

Early the next morning, the stepmother
came to wake up Hansel and Gretel.
"Get up, lazybones," she said.
"We are going into the forest
to cut some wood."

She gave them each a piece of bread.
It was even smaller than before.

Gretel put her bread
in the pocket of her apron.
Hansel put his bread
in the pocket of his coat.

Then they all set out for the forest.

On the way, Hansel crumbled the bread
in his pocket.
Soon he stopped and turned around.
He took out a tiny crumb
and dropped it on the ground.

He stopped again and again.

"Why are you stopping and looking around?"
his father said.

"I am looking at my little white pigeon,"
Hansel said. "She is sitting on our roof
and wants to say good-bye to me."

"Fool!" the stepmother said.
"That is not your little white pigeon.
That is the sun shining on the chimney."

But Hansel was not really looking back
at his little pigeon. He was really
dropping crumbs on the ground.

At last Hansel and Gretel
and their father and stepmother
were deep in the forest.
The children had never seen
this part of the forest before.

The children helped to make a fire.
"The fire will keep you warm, my children,"
the woodcutter said.

"Sit down and rest by the fire,"
the stepmother said. "Your father and I
must go deeper into the forest
to chop some wood.
When our work is done, we will come back
and take you home."

When it was time for lunch,
Gretel took her little piece of bread
out of her apron pocket.
Hansel did not have any bread left,
so Gretel gave him half of hers.

Then the children fell asleep.
And when they woke up, it was dark.

Gretel began to cry.

"Don't cry, little sister," Hansel said.
"The moon is rising now. Soon we will see
the bread crumbs I have dropped.
Then we can find our way home."

The children looked and looked,
but they could not find a single crumb.
The birds had eaten them all!

Hansel and Gretel walked all night.
But they could not find their way
out of the forest.
They walked all the next day
and the morning after that.
And still they could not find their way home.
They were tired and hungry.

And then, suddenly, they saw a little house.

The walls were made of gingerbread.
The roof was made of cake.
The windows were made of sugar candy,
    as clear as glass.

Hansel and Gretel went
    right up to the house and
    began nibbling on it.

Just then a voice called out:

"*Who is there? A bird? A mouse?*
Who is nibbling on my house?"

The children answered:

"*Just the wind in the trees,*
Just the soft forest breeze."

And they went right on eating.

All of a sudden, the door opened.
An old woman came out.
Hansel dropped his piece of roof,
and Gretel dropped her windowpane.

"Don't be afraid, my dears,"
said the old woman. "I will not hurt you.
Come into the house and I will give you
a nice supper."

The old woman gave Hansel and Gretel
some milk to drink and some apple pancakes
with sugar and nuts.

Then she took the children into a little room
with clean white beds.
Hansel and Gretel got into bed
and went to sleep at once.

The children did not know that
the old woman was really a wicked witch —
a witch who ate children.

Early the next morning, the wicked witch
came into the children's room.

She pulled Hansel out of bed
and took him outside.
She put him in a little chicken coop
and banged the door shut.

"You can yell all you want," she said.
"Yell, yell, yell. It won't do you any good."

Then the witch pulled Gretel out of bed.
"Get up, lazybones," she said.
"Your brother is in the chicken coop.
As soon as he is nice and plump
I am going to eat him.
Now get up and make him some breakfast."

Gretel began to cry.
"Cry, cry, cry," said the witch.
"It won't do you any good."

Every day, the witch made Gretel
take food to Hansel so he would get fat.

And every day the witch went out
to the chicken coop
to see if Hansel was fat enough.
"Let me feel your finger, Hansel,"
the witch would say. And each time,
Hansel stuck out a chicken bone.

The old witch could not see very well.
She thought she was feeling Hansel's finger.
But she was really feeling the chicken bone.

After four weeks,
the witch got tired of waiting.
She felt the chicken bone once more and said,
"I don't care if this boy is fat or thin.
Tomorrow I will eat him."

When the witch went away,
Gretel ran over to the chicken coop.
"Don't worry, dear brother," she said.
"I will think of something."

Early the next morning, the witch
came into Gretel's room.
"Get up, lazybones," she said.
"Fill the pot with water and light the fire.
Today I am going to cook your brother
and eat him."

Gretel had to fill the pot and light the fire.

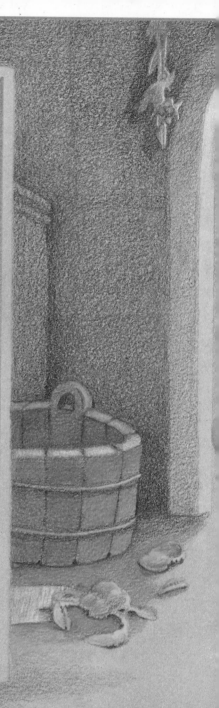

"Now help me bake this bread,"
the witch said.
She pushed Gretel close to the big oven.
"Get in. See if the oven
is hot enough for the bread."

Gretel knew what the wicked witch
was going to do.
The witch is going to bake me in the oven,
Gretel thought. *She is going to eat me, too!*

"Please," said Gretel, "I do not know how
to get inside the oven. How do I get in?"

"Silly goose," the witch said. "It's easy.
Just open the door and get in — like this."
And the witch opened the oven door and
put her head inside.

Quick as a wink, Gretel pushed the witch
into the oven and slammed the door.

Gretel ran to the chicken coop.
"Hansel! Hansel! We are safe!" she shouted.
She opened the chicken coop
and let Hansel out.
"The witch is dead!" she said.
"The witch is dead!"

Hansel and Gretel were so happy
they hugged each other.
"Now we can go home," said Gretel.
But first Hansel wanted to go back
into the witch's house and look around.

The children looked around
and they saw boxes piled in every corner.
They opened one box. It was full of pearls!
They opened another box.
It was full of diamonds!
 They opened one box after another.
 Every box had pearls or diamonds in it.

"These are even nicer than pebbles,"
Hansel said. He filled his pockets
with pearls and diamonds,
and Gretel filled her apron.

Then they set out for home.
They walked until they came to a big lake.
"How will we get across?" Hansel asked.
"There is no bridge, and we have no boat."

"But look!" said Gretel. "I see a white duck
swimming toward us."

And Gretel called to the duck:

"We have no bridge to walk,
No boat to ride.
Pretty white duck, will you take us across
To the other side?"

The white duck came over to the children.
It took them to the other side —
first Hansel and then Gretel.

The children began walking again.
Soon they were in a part of the forest
that they knew.
And then they saw their own house!

They ran the rest of the way,
pushed the door open, and rushed inside.
They were home at last!

The woodcutter was all alone in the house.
His wife had died
while the children were away.
He put his arms around his children
and kissed them.
And they all cried a little bit
because they were so happy.

Then Gretel opened her apron.
All the pearls and diamonds came rolling out.
Hansel pulled a handful of pearls
and diamonds out of his pocket,
and then another and another.
He threw them in the air.

"Now we will have plenty to eat,"
said Hansel.
"Now we will be happy together,"
said Gretel.
And they did live happily after that,
and had plenty to eat.

For Evie, my sister,
with love
—R.B.G.

For Dinah,
who filled the woods
with magic
—W.P.P.

ISBN 0-590-41797-5

Text copyright © 1988 by Ruth Belov Gross.
Illustrations copyright © 1988 by Winslow Pinney Pels.
All rights reserved. Published by Scholastic Inc.

12 11 10 9 8 7 6 5 4 3 2   0 1 2 3/9
Printed in U.S.A.   23
First Scholastic printing, October 1988